KU-224-373

ANIMAL STORIES

by Linda Jennings
adapted by Jackie Andrews

Illustrated by Val Biro

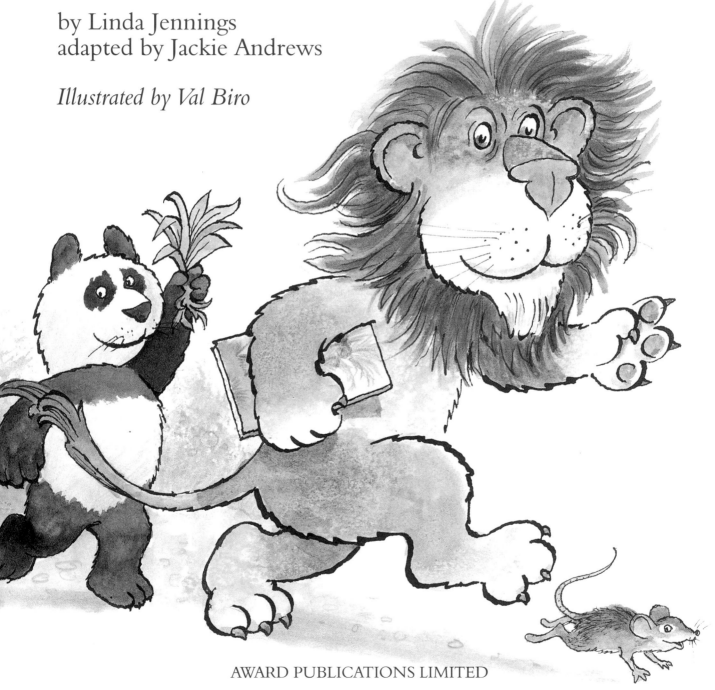

AWARD PUBLICATIONS LIMITED

CONTENTS

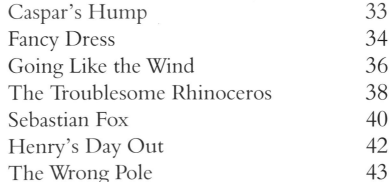

THE LONELY GOAT

There was once a little mountain goat called Tony who was very lonely. So one day he skipped down the mountainside to find a friend. At the bottom was a lake. Tony looked into the water and was surprised to see a little goat exactly like himself.

"Hello!" he bleated joyfully. He bent down to touch the other kid's nose in the water, and immediately the little kid's face dissolved into ripples.

Behind Tony someone laughed loudly and unkindly.

"Ha-ha," chortled Henry, a big grey goat. "What a silly kid you are! Don't you know you're looking at your own reflection? There's no other goat there at all!"

Tony trotted off sadly. He saw plenty of big goats on the mountainside, but couldn't find a little friend.

It was a very tired and lonely little goat that returned home just as the sun was setting.

"There you are, Tony!" cried his father. "You shouldn't have worried your mother and me like that!"

"Where is Mother?" asked Tony.

"We have a big surprise," said Father Goat, "but I'm not sure you deserve it now." But he led Tony to a quiet spot behind the rocks – and there was the big surprise!

A tiny little white kid wobbled beside Mother Goat, on unsteady legs.

"Your little sister!"

Tony bleated happily. He knew he would never be lonely again.

TRACY SPIDER'S BEAUTIFUL WEBS

Tracy Spider could spin the most beautiful webs imaginable and had often won prizes for them.

Unfortunately, humans don't like cobwebs in their houses. They sweep them away as soon as they see them. So Tracy's finest work was often destroyed as soon as it was finished.

Tracy wished she could tell the humans how skilfully she wove her webs and created their intricate patterns.

It was spring-cleaning time: this is the very worst time of the year for house spiders.

Tracy scuttled from one house to another trying to avoid

dusters and vacuum cleaners, until eventually she found a crooked little cottage that looked as if it hadn't ever been spring-cleaned.

She crept under the door, along a dusty corridor, and into a room full of shelves crammed with books and coloured bottles.

Cobwebs hung from every chair, table and shelf!

Tracy found herself a nice dark corner and began to spin lovely, lacy webs.

That evening, the owner of the cottage came home. She was a funny little woman dressed all in black and carrying a broom.

Would she sweep Tracy's lovely webs away with it?

The witch – for that's what she was – stood in the doorway and stared round the room.

"Oh, what beautiful cobwebs!" she exclaimed. Then she saw Tracy sitting anxiously in her latest web. "I do believe they are the best webs I've ever seen! Will you stay with me, little spider?"

And Tracy, happy at last to find someone who appreciated her work, was glad to make her home with the little witch.

THE PONY PUP

"Let's call him Midge," said Tim's mum, looking at the tiny puppy Dad had brought home under his coat.

"Chap at work said he'd have to be put down," said Dad. "No one wanted him."

Poor little Midge was the runt of the litter. He was like a little rabbit, with a downy grey coat and long floppy ears.

"He's got very big paws though," said Tim. "That usually means a big dog."

But big paws or not, Midge was there to stay.

At three months, Midge was the size of a small terrier.

At four months, he was as big as a spaniel.

At six months he looked a bit like a Labrador with long ears.

And by the time he was a year old Midge was as big as an Irish wolfhound. And still he grew.

"Midge seems to be a stupid name for him now," said Dad. But Midge knew his name and somehow it suited him.

"He's not a dog, he's a pony," said Tim's little cousin, Betsy, as she rode on Midge's back.

"He's a pony-dog," said Tim, proudly.

Everyone loved Midge, even if he did sometimes knock people over with a wag of his tail, or leave huge muddy paw marks on the kitchen floor. He could carry a big basket of shopping from the supermarket, pull Dad's golf clubs round the golf course, and even jump over fences, like a gymkhana pony.

Midge was everybody's pony-dog!

KITTY SMARTYPANTS

Kerry noticed the little cat on her way home from school one day. It was black, with a little white face, four white paws, and big green eyes.

"Oooh, isn't it sweet!" cried Kerry.

"Best leave it alone," said Kerry's mum. "It probably belongs to the people on the other side of the hedge."

But Kerry thought about the little cat all the way home. She felt sure it wanted to come with her. She kept turning round to look back down the road to see if it was following, but all she saw was shadows.

That night it was very warm, and Kerry left her bedroom window open. She went to bed and was soon fast asleep.

When she woke up, Kerry found she couldn't move her feet. Something was sitting on them! She looked down the bed and was not at all surprised to see the little black cat curled up on the duvet.

"I knew you wanted to come and live with me," said Kerry, stroking the little cat's head. "I'm going to call you Kitty Smartypants, because you knew exactly where to find me." The little cat purred and purred.

Kerry's mother asked all their neighbours if they knew who had lost a little black cat with a white face, but no one could help her. So Kitty Smartypants lived happily with Kerry and her mum for many years.

EGG HUNT

Matilda Hen was a very good layer. She would sometimes lay ten eggs a week. But was Farmer Dixon pleased with her? No! For Matilda would lay one egg in the barn, one under the hedge and maybe one in Annie Dixon's dolls' pram. Anywhere but in one of the nice nesting boxes in Farmer Dixon's hencoop.

Annie didn't mind. She enjoyed playing "Hunt the eggs".

But Farmer Dixon *did* mind. He didn't have time to hunt all over the farm for Matilda's eggs.

"She'll have to go," he said.

Now Matilda was Annie's favourite hen and Annie didn't want to lose her. And when she saw Matilda strutting crossly from the noisy henhouse one day, Annie suddenly realised just what was wrong.

"You want some peace and quiet, don't you, Matilda?"

Matilda clucked and disappeared under the hawthorn hedge to lay another egg.

Annie got an old orange box from the barn. She lined it with straw and placed it in the shade of a willow tree, where it was completely hidden. It was just what Matilda wanted.

Now she goes off to her own special nesting box and lays a complete batch of eggs. It's a secret only Matilda and the Dixons know about. After all, it wouldn't do for all the other hens to discover it, would it?

14

THE THIRD LITTLE PIG

In the story of the Three Little Pigs, one little pig outwitted the Big Bad Wolf, if you remember, by building a sturdy little house of bricks.

Unfortunately, this third little pig grew terribly bigheaded. Strutting around with his head in the air, he boasted, "I'm a very clever pig. I don't need anyone's help or advice."

Now one day a man came to live right next door to the third little pig. He was big and red-faced, and drove a white van. His name was Joe Cleaver. As soon as he saw the third little pig, Joe came round to introduce himself.

"Pleased to meet you," said the third little pig. "I expect you've heard all about me and how tremendously clever I am."

"Yes, indeed," said Joe. "A most ingenious pig – and so deliciously plump!"

The third little pig was so puffed up with pride that he didn't see there was something rather sinister about that last remark.

Very soon he and his new neighbour were the best of friends.

"Come to supper with me tonight," said Joe one day.

"Delighted!" said the third little pig.

All the afternoon he could hear Joe's preparations for the meal. There was a lot of clattering of plates, and the sound of a big knife being sharpened.

Just as the third little pig was polishing his trotters, there was a knock at his door.

"Little pig, little pig, let me come in!" cried a voice.

"Not by the hair on my chinny-chin-chin," said the third little pig, just as he had once said to the Big Bad Wolf.

"Don't be stupid, little pig," growled Dandy Dog. "It's only me, and it's very important."

"Oh, very well," said the third little pig, and he opened the door. "But you must be quick because I've been invited out to supper next door."

"That's just it," yelped Dandy Dog. "You must not go!"

"Why ever not?" asked the third little pig. "Mr Cleaver has invited me because I'm a very special and important pig."

"You'll be no sort of pig at all if you go there," retorted Dandy Dog. "You'll be bacon and sausages. That's what I came to tell you. Joe Cleaver has just opened a shop in the village. He's a butcher!"

"Oh dear." The third little pig gulped. He trembled from head to foot. Then he remembered the remark about how deliciously plump he was, and the sound of the knife being sharpened.

Straight away, he packed his bags and moved out. He built a new house of bricks somewhere else, and stopped boasting about how clever he was.

The third little pig became a quieter, more modest pig and was very glad he had listened to a real friend.

MOTORWAY DOG

Pippin crouched underneath the hedge, trembling. Hundreds of cars and lorries kept rushing past, making the hedge shake, and the air was full of petrol fumes.

When she was a puppy, Pippin had been very happy. But the family had grown tired of her and decided they didn't want her any more. So Pippin was bundled into the car and when they were far enough from home, they pushed her out on to the grass verge and drove away.

Frightened and hungry, Pippin squeezed through the hedge and into a field, away from the sound of the traffic.

Something huge and brown snorted at her.

"What are you doing in my field?"

"I was l…left here," said Pippin.

The big brown bull sighed. He'd come across abandoned dogs before and knew how heartless some humans could be.

Just then, another car stopped by the hedge.

"There's a nice field for our picnic," piped a small voice.

"No it isn't, stupid! There's a bull in it!" said another.

"The next field looks all right," said their mother, and the family climbed over the gate carrying a hamper and chairs.

"You're in luck," said the bull to Pippin. "There's a nice family for you. I can always tell. Just sit near them and look pathetic."

18

Pippin thanked him and squeezed under the fence. The family was already spreading out their picnic. It smelled quite delicious. Pippin's mouth drooled. Sausage rolls! Ham sandwiches! Chicken legs!

She padded up to the little girl, whining softly.

"Oh, what a nice dog!"

"No collar," said Dad. "Looks hungry, too."

"I bet some horrible person threw her from their car," said the boy.

The children's mother held a piece of chicken out to the little dog. Pippin stepped forward, wagging her tail, and gently took the tasty morsel delicately in her mouth. It was gone in two bites.

"She's lovely," said the little girl. "Can we take her home with us? *Please*."

"Well, we can't leave her here," said Mum. "Not with that motorway so near. It's too dangerous."

So when the family packed up their things and returned to the car, Pippin went with them. As soon as the car door opened, she sprang inside and lay down on the floor.

"Motorway dog," said the little girl. "You're ours now."

And Pippin gave one big happy sigh.

THE CHATTERBOX

Mrs Peasbody was a chatterbox. She talked morning, noon and night about everything and everybody. And if her husband wouldn't listen to her, she talked to the dog, to the cat and even to the plants.

One day Farmer Griffiths came to the door.

"Oh, Farmer Griffiths," cried Mrs Peasbody. "Fancy seeing you, I was just saying to George…"

"Mrs Peasbody," Farmer Griffiths interrupted quickly, "I was wondering if I could rent your field for my donkey."

"Of course," said Mrs Peasbody. "Which reminds me…"

But Farmer Griffiths didn't stop to listen. He fetched his little donkey and put him in the Peasbodys' field, then hurried back to his farm.

Now one day in summer, when just about everybody had gone away on holiday, for the first time in weeks Mrs Peasbody found she had no one to talk to. So she took off her apron, picked up a big bunch of juicy carrots, and went down to the bottom of the garden to talk to the donkey.

Two hours later, Mrs Peasbody was still talking. The little donkey had munched all the carrots and began to nod his head at the sound of her voice going on and on and on…

Suddenly, he fell over.

"Oh, whatever's the matter?" cried Mrs Peasbody. "I'd better tell Farmer Griffiths."

"Goodness gracious," said Farmer Griffiths when he saw the donkey. "He's got no back legs."

20

"They were there this morning," said Mrs Peasbody. "I went to talk to him and took him a bunch of carrots. Perhaps someone's stolen them."

The farmer took the little donkey to the vet.

"Hmm, no legs," said the vet. "If you ask me he's suffering from a severe case of overfeeding with conversation. Haven't you ever heard of people talking the hind legs off a donkey?"

"Is it curable?" Farmer Griffiths asked anxiously.

"Plenty of rest and no noise," prescribed the vet, putting some earplugs inside the donkey's long ears.

Poor Mrs Peasbody was so upset when she heard what had happened to the little donkey that she hardly said anything for a week, and after that she only spoke when she had something important to say.

And the little donkey's legs grew back again as good as new.

THE BIG FRIGHT

A family of frogs once lived in a beautiful garden pond. It had green wavy weed, waterlilies, and a little stone statue pouring water from an urn. Round the edges there were flat stones and flowering plants.

One day the owners of the pond came and put something new in the pond. The frogs disappeared amongst the waterlilies until the humans had gone, then one bold little frog popped out of the water to take a look.

Very soon he dived down again, shaking with fright.

"There's a horrible big bird up there," he cried, "with a wicked-looking beak and long spindly legs."

22

"That sounds like a heron," said an old frog. "Herons eat frogs."

The frogs hid under the water and croaked mournfully.

But the bold little frog could not resist having another peek.

"It's still there," he told the others. "It hasn't moved."

"No," said the old frog. "Herons stay very still until a frog swims near them, then *swish, crunch*! That's the end of the frog."

The bold little frog was very annoyed.

"We'll see about that," he said to himself. "I'll give that heron such a fright, he'll go away for good!" – and he swam up behind the bird and leaped straight up on to its back!

But he didn't land on warm feathers. Oh no. Instead he slid all the way down a cold metal slide and splashed back into the pond.

"It's not a real bird at all!" he told the other frogs. "It's made of metal!"

The frogs swam to the surface to see for themselves, and soon they were leaping and splashing all over the metal heron.

And one bold frog even perched on its wicked-looking beak!

THE DANCING BEAR

Many, many years ago there was a dancing bear called Bobo. He travelled to all the towns and villages with his master, Frederick, and while Frederick played his flute, Bobo danced. Frederick wasn't a bad master; he fed Bobo well and groomed his thick coat so it shone.

But Bobo was not happy. He remembered when he was cub, living in a big leafy forest beside a swift-flowing river, with a lush meadow beyond. He remembered playing with the other cubs, and snuggling up to his mother when he slept.

One day some men had come and captured Bobo in a big net and carried him away. He had been sold to Frederick, who kept Bobo on a heavy iron chain and trained him to dance.

Although the big brown bear did just as he was told and even allowed people to feed and fuss him, he always looked sad.

One day Frederick and Bobo came to a little town on top of a hill. They were going to a fair being held in the meadow below the castle.

The meadow led down to a river, and beyond it was a forest.

As soon as Bobo saw it, something stirred in him. Could this be his old home?

Bobo danced as his master played the flute, but his thoughts were far away.

Just then a wasp stung Frederick on his hand and he dropped the iron chain.

Bobo was free!

The crowd scattered in alarm as Bobo ran down the meadow as fast as he could. He lumbered across the river and didn't stop running until he was deep inside the forest and could no longer hear the sound of human voices.

Bobo was home!

THE DUCK'S MOTHER

When Rosie was a tiny little duckling she lost her mother. Gemma found her one day, staggering by the pond, cheeping frantically.

Gemma searched round the pond and in the reeds, but she couldn't find a duck that was looking for a duckling. So she took Rosie home with her.

Gemma made a comfy bed for Rosie out of an old shoebox. She put the box on the draining-board and filled the sink with water: her own warm bed and safe little pond.

"We'll have to find somewhere else for her to live," said Gemma's mother.

Because Rosie was so young, she thought Gemma was her mother. The little duckling followed her everywhere, and became distressed when Gemma disappeared on school days. But when Gemma came home, Rosie would be waiting for her by the gate.

One day Gemma left home in a hurry and didn't shut the gate properly. She didn't notice Rosie follow her down the road. But when she reached the school gates she saw all her friends laughing and pointing.

"There's a duck following you, Gemma!"

Just for that day, Gemma was allowed to keep Rosie in the classroom with her. She behaved very well, but as the teacher pointed out, "If Rosie is allowed to come to school every day, then everyone will want to bring their pets. Then where would we be?" she added. But most of the children thought school would be much more fun with their pets around.

Once Rosie was fully grown, Gemma took her back to the pond.

"She won't want to stay," thought Gemma sadly. "She'll follow me home again."

But when they reached the pond they found a handsome drake there. He waddled up to Rosie and fluffed out his feathers. Without a backward glance, Rosie hopped into the water to swim with her new friend.

A few months later, Gemma opened the back door to find Rosie outside – with seven little ducklings.

She stayed long enough for Gemma to admire her family, then off she went down the garden, her little ducklings following behind.

THE LAZY SQUIRREL

It was the most beautiful autumn that any of the animals of Fairweather Wood could remember.

But there was no time to just sit and enjoy the warm sunshine: all the squirrels had to work hard to find nuts for their winter stores.

All except Dudley.

"Enjoy the good weather while it lasts," he told them. "There's plenty of time to forage."

He spent his own days lazily basking in the sun or snoozing amongst the branches of the trees. Occasionally he would pick up the odd acorn, but generally he didn't bother.

"Work, work, work, that's all you think of!" he complained to the other squirrels.

By the end of October the weather turned cold and the days grew short and grey.

Dudley decided it was time to go looking for nuts. He was expecting to find lots of acorns and hazelnuts fallen from the trees, but as he searched amongst the fallen leaves, he quickly realised that the other squirrels had taken them all.

"What am I going to do?" Dudley wondered. "I don't have enough food to last all winter. If only I hadn't been so lazy!"

Fortunately, the other squirrels took pity on him and shared their spare nuts with him.

All the same, it was a long, hard, winter – especially for Dudley.

At the very first signs of spring, Dudley was up and about helping his friends to build their dreys. He was determined never to be lazy again.

NESTING TIME

It was St Valentine's Day, and Mr and Mrs Robin were looking for somewhere to build their nest.

Mrs Robin was very difficult to please. The old kettle in the ditch had a hole in it and she didn't fancy the letterbox on the corner. People would drop letters on them.

"How about this nice scarecrow's pocket?" asked Mr Robin.

"Too ordinary," said Mrs Robin. "Everyone builds nests in scarecrows' pockets."

Mr Robin flew here and there, trying to find somewhere to please Mrs Robin. Then, just as he was about to give up, he found the perfect place.

It stood large and square on the floor of the shed and it even had a glass window in the front of it.

Busily the two birds built their nest and Mrs Robin was soon sitting on a clutch of eggs. She looked out of the window and tut-tutted at all the mess – lots of wire and metal lying all over the floor.

One day the shed door opened and a young man came in.

He started to gather together all the bits and pieces lying all over the floor. "It's about time I put this all together again," he muttered. Then he reached for Mrs Robin's new home.

"Oh no!" he cried. "Mary!"

The young man's wife looked in at the door. "What's the matter?"

"There's a robin's nest in the television!"

"How lovely!" she said. "You'll just have to mend it after the baby robins have flown away."

"Real live robins on the box!" joked her husband. "Much better than a nature film."

THE SHORT AND THE TALL

William was a great big Irish wolfhound, and Danny was a dachshund. They were great friends: they shared the same basket and even the same food bowl. But when it came to going for a walk they had a problem.

Long-legged William could run like the wind, but poor Danny, with his little short legs, just couldn't keep up.

And William could see right across the park to the wood, with its deer and rabbits, and a wide lake that was splendid to swim in. But Danny couldn't see any of these wonderful things.

He was always tired out before he'd gone even halfway across the park.

So William would go off, leaving Danny to sniff around the bushes or play with other small dogs like himself.

One day, when Danny chased a ball into the shrubbery, he found something very exciting. It was a skateboard! Danny had often seen the children riding these boards, and he knew they could go very fast.

It gave him an idea.

When William came back from his long walk, he helped Danny push the skateboard all the way home with his nose.

They attached a piece of string to one end of it, and then Danny climbed aboard. William took the end of the string in his mouth and pulled little Danny all the way to the park – and right across to the lake at the far end.

It was wonderful. Danny explored the woods with William, chased rabbits and paddled in the shallow waters of the lake.

After that, there wasn't anywhere that William and Danny couldn't go. They even went all the way to Scotland to visit the Loch Ness Monster!

CASPAR'S HUMP

One morning, Caspar the camel woke up feeling very grumpy. He didn't want his breakfast, and he didn't want to give rides to children.

"My, you have got the hump this morning," said Ted the elephant.

"Very funny – I don't think!" grumbled Caspar.

"You have got the hump this morning," said Jenny his keeper, when Caspar grumbled about kneeling down for the children to climb on his back.

"He hasn't got one hump," said one child, laughing. "He's got two!"

Caspar was so fed up with their jokes that he refused to kneel down.

The Head Keeper came up to see what was wrong.

"Caspar's got the hump," explained Jenny.

"That's a pity," said the Head Keeper, "because I was going to send him to the new safari park. He'd be much happier there. But they won't want a camel with the hump."

Safari park? Caspar had heard how much nicer it was than the zoo. Slowly he sank down on to his knees and let the children climb on to his back.

"That's better," said Jenny. "Caspar's hump has completely disappeared."

"But he's still got two on his back," said the children.

Everybody laughed – even Caspar.

FANCY DRESS

"Delilah Duck is having a fancy dress party," said Maxie Mouse, reading the notice pinned on the big oak tree.

The animals were very excited. There weren't many parties in Oakapple Wood. They soon decided what costumes they were going to wear.

All except Harriet Hedgehog, who burst into tears.

"I can't dress up as anything," she wailed. "How can a hedgehog wear clothes over these prickles? They'd poke through the material. I'd look silly."

Harriet shuffled away sadly, until she came to the Baxters' ￼en. John and Anne were having a birthday party. Harriet ￼uld see all kinds of delicious food spread on the table under

34

the apple tree: sausages, crisps, sandwiches and… what was that? It looked like a hedgehog! But then she saw that it was really half a grapefruit covered with little sticks. On the end of each stick was a little cube of cheese or pineapple.

Suddenly, Harriet had an idea for her fancy dress costume.

The evening of Delilah Duck's party was perfect. Little stars twinkled in the sky and there was a huge yellow moon lighting up the wood.

Everyone admired Maxie's Mickey Mouse costume, and ory abbit's Peter abbit costume. Basil Badger came dressed as a clown.

But then a very strange-looking creature arrived. It was Harriet Hedgehog! She wore acorns stuck all over her prickles.

"I'm a party treat for squirrels," she announced.

It was such an original outfit, she won first prize.

And the squirrels had a wonderful time eating all those acorns!

GOING LIKE THE WIND

Lion had a great idea. "We'll run a race," he told the animals in the game reserve. "The winner will have free food gathered by all the other animals for a whole year."

It took a lot of sorting out. To make the race as fair as possible, the small and slow animals were placed at different points along the racetrack.

And because Cheetah was the fastest animal of them all, he was put right back behind the starting line, even further back than the zebras, leopards, antelopes and wildebeests.

Lion lined all the animals up in position.

"All ready? Get set, GO!" he roared and the race began.

Mrs Lion was at the finishing post to record the winner. She didn't know why she should bother, since the winner was bound to be Cheetah.

She gave a big, bored yawn and just then felt a sudden gust of wind and the earth tremble.

"What was *that*?" she wondered.

Not long afterwards, little Antelope galloped past the finishing post. "The winner!" shouted Mrs Lion.

Antelope was delighted to think she wouldn't have to search for food for a whole year.

But where was Cheetah? Had he got lost? No one had seen him since the beginning of the race.

That night the animals all celebrated with a party and brought their gifts to the winner. Quiet, gentle Antelope was popular with everyone. Suddenly, who should arrive but Cheetah, looking tired and sore-footed. "I've run miles," he complained. "And Antelope isn't really the winner – I am!"

Cheetah explained that he'd been running so fast that he had overshot the winning-post and couldn't stop until he ran into a water hole.

Mrs Lion could remember the sudden wind and shaking earth. "So that was Cheetah," she said.

But no one wanted to take the prize away from Antelope.

"It's no good being fast if you can't stop," declared Lion.

And everyone agreed.

THE TROUBLESOME RHINOCEROS

There was once a group of jungle animals that got on remarkably well with each other.

As King of the Jungle, Lion made sure everyone in his little group behaved themselves. "It's so nice to see everyone being friendly towards each other," he said.

Now one day, while the animals were dozing in the midday sun, they heard the thump-thump-thump of a very heavy animal galloping towards them.

Lion opened one eye and saw an enormous rhinoceros thundering through the trees. He had a wickedly sharp horn and looked very fierce indeed.

"Can we help you?" asked Lion.

"I'm Rhino," said the rhinoceros, "and I've come to join you."

"I see," said Lion, slowly. "And what do you do best?" For every animal that wanted to join the little group had to prove they'd be useful.

"I can charge!" said Rhino. "I can trample everyone underfoot and I can stab things with my sharp horn."

"We don't need anyone like that," said Elephant. "We all live in peace here – we don't want anyone troublesome."

"Peace?" roared Rhino. "How very boring!" And he wheeled around in disgust and charged off through the trees.

Suddenly all the animals heard a loud *scrunch*, followed by silence.

"What was that?" asked Monkey. She swung away to have a look, but was soon back, chuckling merrily.

"Come and see!" she said to the others.

The animals followed her through the jungle to an enormous tree. There, with his big horn stuck firmly in the trunk, was Rhino.

"Can anyone help me?" he said, plaintively. "I'm stuck."

"I could help you," said Elephant. "But first you must promise never to charge through our jungle again."

Rhino promised. Elephant curled his long trunk round Rhino's middle and pulled. Out came the horn and Rhino stood there looking relieved.

After that, Rhino was as good as his word. And he only used his horn for spearing fruit for the monkeys and parrots.

SEBASTIAN FOX

"Why are foxes always shown as nasty, sneaky creatures?" Sebastian Fox asked himself one day. "I'm not like that at all. I'm nice, honest and friendly."

He decided he would try to prove it.

First he went to see Farmer Baxter's chickens.

"Hello," said Sebastian, through the wire. "I'm a friendly fox, you know. Just let me prove it."

"That's what they all say," said the cockerel. "Look what happened to poor Priscilla. Gone in a flash, she was, in the jaws of someone just like you."

Suddenly there was a loud *bang* and a bullet whistled past Sebastian's ear.

"Missed him!" cried Farmer Baxter. "Pity."

Sebastian ran away as fast as he could.

Eventually, he came to the kennels where the Holloby Hunt hounds lived. As soon as they smelled Sebastian they began barking furiously.

"Grrr! A fox! Just let us out of here. We'll get him!"

"Please," shouted Sebastian over their noise. "I just want to be friends."

But the dogs had been trained to chase foxes, and that's just what they wanted to do.

Sebastian made his way sadly back to his den.

A party of school children saw him.

"Look, Miss, a fox!" said one of them. "Isn't he beautiful?"

"Shh," said the teacher. "We don't want to scare him, do we? Yes, you can take a photo, Donna. And you can all make pictures of him when we get back, for the classroom wall."

Sebastian stood very still, his fine bushy tail fluffed out and his head held high.

Snap! went the camera, then the children moved on, still talking about the handsome fox they had seen.

Sebastian Fox felt very proud and happy. He was loved and admired, and his picture was going up on a classroom wall. What more could a fox wish for?

HENRY'S DAY OUT

Henry Hamster lived in a cage in Mary Brown's conservatory, where he had a good view of the garden. He had a little wheel he could run round in for exercise.

When Mary left the cage door unlatched one day, Henry thought he'd like to explore the garden. It didn't take him long to find a way down to the floor and under the conservatory door. Hamsters are good at things like that.

But what looked very attractive from the safety of his cage, was rather frightening when he was actually out there. Everything was so big!

Henry twitched his nose and smelled the new-mown grass of the lawn, and the rose blooms. As he made his way towards the rose bed, wondering if roses could be eaten, Henry suddenly smelled something else. He'd smelled it before when he was safely in his cage in the conservatory. It was a cat.

Now Tomkins the cat looked big and fierce to Henry from inside his cage. Out here in the rose bed, Tomkins was huge and terrifying. Henry cowered down, pretending to be a stone.

But Tomkins was not fooled. *Wham*! A big furry paw pinned poor Henry to the ground.

"*Tomkins*! What have you got there?"

That was Mary, sounding very cross. Tomkins sped off guiltily across the lawn towards the house, leaving Henry behind.

Gently, Mary picked up her quaking little hamster.

"How on earth did you get out here?" she asked. "Never mind, we'll put you back in your own little cage. You'll be much safer there."

And Henry was only too glad to be home again!

THE WRONG POLE

Peter was drawing a snowy picture of penguins sitting on ice floes. On a particularly big island of ice he had drawn a polar bear.

When the teacher looked over his shoulder she said:

"You've drawn that beautifully, Peter – but I'm afraid it's wrong. You see, polar bears don't live with penguins. Polar bears come from the North Pole; penguins live at the South Pole."

Peter frowned. He liked his picture and didn't want to rub out his polar bear just because it didn't belong there. Instead, he took it home with him and stood it on top of his bedroom cupboard.

That night, Peter dreamed his picture had come to life.

Above the howling wind and the clatter of penguins, he could hear a very unhappy, growly sound. It was the polar bear.

"I don't like it here," said the polar bear.

"Why not?" asked Peter. "It's just as snowy and icy as the North Pole."

"But I'm *lonely*," said the polar bear. "There aren't any other bears here. I want to go home."

Peter sat down beside the polar bear and wondered what to do. It was a very long way to the North Pole. But it was his fault that the polar bear was lonely.

And then Peter woke up.

He saw his picture on the cupboard, and he knew exactly what he had to do.

Peter got out his box of paints. He took his picture and carefully painted out the polar bear with white paint. Then he took another sheet of paper and drew another snowy scene, but this time he drew a family of polar bears! And one of them was smiling, as if to say "thank you."

FRED THE RACING DONKEY

Fred the donkey lived in a meadow next to a field of proud racehorses that were always bragging about the races they had won.

Fred liked to imagine he could race, too, and tried to keep up with them as they cantered along the fence. But they only laughed at him as they galloped away.

"I wish I could win an important race," sighed Fred. "That would show them!"

Early one morning young Ben from the farm came to see Fred.

"We've got a big surprise for you, Fred," he said, giving him a carrot. "Just wait and see."

A big surprise? What could it be? Fred began to feel very excited.

Then Lucy came with a curry-comb and a brush. She groomed Fred's coat until it shone. Then she saddled him up, opened the gate and led him down the lane to a field on the other side of the farm.

It was filled with people and donkeys. Fred had never seen so many.

Ben stuck a number 7 on Fred's saddle, and Lucy helped him mount up. He leaned forward to whisper in Fred's silky ear. "Do your best for us, Fred, won't you."

Fred trotted up to a line of donkeys waiting patiently in a row.

"What's happening?" he asked.

"It's the Donkey Derby," said his neighbour. "A special race just for us donkeys. Haven't you heard of it?"

Fred had only heard about a horse race called the Derby. One of the racehorses never stopped bragging about winning it.

This was Fred's chance! He'd show those horses. He'd win the Donkey Derby!

Someone blew a whistle and they were off.

"Come on, Fred!" urged Ben.

Fred thought about the racehorses thundering over the turf. He gathered speed, passing one donkey after another until there was only one in front of him…

"FRED IS COMING UP FAST!" shouted the race commentator. "THEY'RE NECK-AND-NECK AS THEY COME UP TO THE FINISHING POST! AND IT'S FRED FIRST. DAISY SECOND. FRED IS THE WINNER OF THIS YEAR'S DONKEY DERBY!"

Later that evening, Fred trotted up to the fence, proudly wearing his red rosette.

"I won a race!" he told the horses.

"Bet it's a race no one ever heard of," said one.

"Yes they have," said Fred. "I won the Derby."

TIMOTHY TIGER

Timothy Tiger's uncle was famous. He starred in television adverts watched by millions of people.

"It's made him very rich," boasted Timothy to the other tigers.

"What does a tiger want with money?" they said. "What's your uncle got that we haven't, here in the safari park?"

"He's got *fame*," said Timothy. "Not like me. I'm just the nephew of the famous tiger." And he went off to sulk.

Life in the park was very comfortable but dull: eating and sleeping and watching people drive by in their cars, taking photographs.

There wasn't much chance of becoming famous.

Timothy stretched out under a tree and dozed. After a while, something tickled his nose. "*Atishoo!*" he sneezed. He opened his eyes and saw a very small boy in red dungarees goggling at him.

Now, Timothy was really a gentle tiger. He guessed the little boy had wandered away from his family. Gently he picked him up by his dungarees and carried him out from the bushes.

There was a car parked beside the road. As soon as Timothy appeared, a woman shrieked, "Norman! That tiger's got our Kevin!"

The man flapped his arms at Timothy and made shooing noises.

"Silly things," thought Timothy. He put Kevin down on the grass.

48

"Thank you, Mr Tiger," said Kevin, stroking Timothy's nose. Timothy licked him with his big rough tongue.

"Oh – he's brought my baby back to me!" sobbed Kevin's mum. "A tiger has rescued my little boy!"

After that, the newspaper and television people came to see Timothy the friendly tiger. They took his photograph and filmed him with Kevin hugging him.

Timothy appeared on the early evening news and in all the morning papers next day.

So many people flocked to the park to see him that Timothy found it hard to get a moment's peace and quiet away from the crowds.

It wasn't long before he began to tire of all the excitement and fame. And when someone suggested that they should take him up to London to make a film, Timothy hid among the trees and couldn't be found.

"I've changed my mind," said Timothy. 'I don't think I want to be famous after all."

THE MAGICIAN'S RABBIT

eg was a magician's rabbit. He knew just how to hide himself so that when Alfonso, the magician, pulled him out of a hat, it looked like magic.

"But it's just a trick," thought eg. "It's not magic at all. I wish I was really a magic rabbit."

It happened that just then a witch flew by. Just what eg needed!

"Hello, witch!" he called. "Can you help me?"

The witch smiled at eg with her crooked smile. "You're the magician's rabbit," she said.

"But I'm not really magic," said eg, "and the children know it. One little boy even said he knew how my trick was done. He was a real clever-stick."

"Was he now?" said the witch. "Well, we'll give him something to wonder about." And she muttered some magic words over eg.

That evening, at a children's party, eg sprang out of Alfonso's hat as usual. The little clever-stick was there too, and he called out rudely:

"That old trick's *boring*. It's not magic!"

eg drew himself up and started to grow and grow. Soon he was the same size as the boy.

"Help!" cried the child. "It's a monster rabbit!" All the children squealed and rushed towards the door.

Poor Alfonso was very worried. He didn't want a monster rabbit. He'd never get asked to entertain at any more children's parties.

But just as the boy reached the door, eg shrank back to his normal size.

"I'm sorry, children," said eg. "I didn't mean to frighten you. I'm not really a monster rabbit."

"Wow!" cried the children. "A talking rabbit! That's real magic!"

51

PANDA FRIENDS

Polly was a giant panda. She was the children's favourite animal in the safari park.

Now there aren't many giant pandas left in the world, and certainly Polly was the only one in the park.

"Wouldn't you like a panda friend, Polly?" the children asked.

But Polly didn't think she would. She had her own little house, all the bamboo shoots she could possibly want, and the children thought she was special. Another panda might spoil things.

"I've a surprise for you, Polly," said her keeper one day. "Moscow Zoo has sent us a special present. What do you suppose it is?"

It was another panda. And Polly knew that she would dislike him on sight.

The new panda arrived the next day. He was called Boris.

"You have a beautiful place, Miss Polly," said Boris. "It is good to be here."

Polly turned her back on Boris and munched furiously on her bamboo shoots which she'd piled at the back of her house for herself.

"Ooh, look!" cried the children. "Polly doesn't like him. Polly's sulking."

Polly knew she was being unfriendly and rude. But the more the children scolded her, the worse she became.

Boris gazed up at the children with sad panda eyes.

"He's awfully upset. You are horrible, Polly."

And so it went on. Boris was so well-mannered that he didn't complain when Polly took all the bamboo into her corner and ate the lot. But he began to look thin and sickly, while Polly grew fatter and fatter.

Eventually, the keeper put Polly in a cage on her own, while Boris was free to roam around and enjoy the children's attention. But he didn't look happy, and Polly began to feel very lonely indeed.

One day, as Boris went by her cage, she put out a paw and touched his nose.

"Sorry, Boris," she mumbled. "I've been a very naughty, selfish panda."

And Boris, being the good fellow he was, forgave her willingly.

After that, they became good friends and lived happily together for many years.

FLOPSY'S ESCAPE

Flopsy was a beautiful, black, lop-eared rabbit. He lived in a hutch in a big wild garden and every day he was let out to run around.

One day he looked out of his hutch and saw a whole family of strange rabbits on the lawn. They were all brown and their ears stood straight up. "There must be something wrong with them," thought Flopsy. "Next time I go out for a run, I'll find where they live."

Imagine his surprise when he saw dozens of other rabbits in the field at the bottom of the garden, all feeding and playing in the early evening sunshine. And every rabbit was brown with sticking-up ears!

Then the wild rabbits spotted Flopsy and crowded round him. "What on earth is it?" asked one.

"I'm a rabbit," said Flopsy. "Just like you."

"You're not a bit like us," said another. "Whoever heard of a black rabbit with ears drooping down to the ground?"

All the wild rabbits laughed.

"He's one of those posh foreign rabbits," said a rough-looking buck. "That's why he's different." He bared his big front teeth at Flopsy and thumped his back feet in warning. "Hop back to your hutch and be quick about it!"

Poor Flopsy turned and fled. But before he hopped back into his garden he took one last look at the unfriendly wild rabbits.

"They're different from me, too," he said. "But I don't mind."

There was a rustle in the bushes and a little wild doe rabbit suddenly hopped out.

"They're only jealous," she told Flopsy. "I think you are very handsome."

And she stayed with Flopsy all day, playing hide-and-seek and tag and sharing dandelions with him.

Flopsy and his new friend played together every evening. Very gradually other young rabbits came over to join them in the garden. And before long, they all forgot that Flopsy was a bit different from them.

A rabbit is a rabbit, after all.

GOLDILOCKS' BROTHER

There once was a family of bears who lived in the middle of a wood. One day they were going to visit their cousin on the other side of the wood.

"Come on, Baby Bear!" his parents called impatiently.

Baby Bear dropped the wasp trap he was making and ran downstairs.

"Have you closed your window?" asked Father Bear, but Baby Bear had already scooted down the path ahead of his parents. And of course he hadn't closed his window.

Now, ever since a girl called Goldilocks had messed up their house and eaten their breakfast, they always made sure the door and windows were locked before they went out.

As soon as the bears had gone, a small boy called Barney crept out of the bushes. He looked just like his sister, and her name was Goldilocks.

Ever since she had come home with her story about the Three Bears, Barney had wanted to visit their house himself and see the chairs, bowls and beds in all three different sizes.

Barney now climbed up a tree and squeezed in through Baby Bear's bedroom window. Unfortunately, he stepped right on to the wasp trap that Baby Bear had been making before he went out, and tipped honey everywhere.

Carefully, Barney made his way across the landing. But his shoes were slippery with honey. At the top of the stairs his feet went from under him and Barney tumbled all the way down to the bottom. He lay dazed and bruised, feeling very foolish.

Just then, Mother Bear opened the front door, having discovered that Baby Bear hadn't closed his window after all. Baby Bear peered round her at the sticky little boy at the foot of their stairs.

"Who's been and broken my wasp trap?" he cried.

Then, just like Goldilocks, Barney leaped to his feet and ran out of the cottage and all the way home.

WANDA WITCH'S NEW KITTEN

One day Nigel the wizard went to visit his old friend, Wanda Witch, and brought her a present: a ginger kitten.

Now Wanda was far too polite to say so, but she didn't really want the little ginger kitten. True, she needed a new cat since her last one had died – but a *ginger* kitten! Everyone knew that a witch's cat had to be black.

She would be the laughing-stock of all the other witches.

But the ginger kitten followed Wanda into the kitchen and wound himself round her legs. Grudgingly Wanda put down a saucer of food and the kitten ate the lot.

Wanda then fetched a paint-brush and a large tin of special black dye. She would try and dye the kitten black.

But the ginger kitten didn't like being painted with the horrible black stuff. He ran off and hid himself in the herb garden. Nothing would make him come out, not even another saucer of food.

Wanda Witch called and called her new kitten in vain and finally went to bed. She had to admit that it was nice to have a cat again. She wanted her kitten to come in and curl up beside her, and keep her company.

That night it rained heavily. "Poor little kitten," thought Wanda. "He'll get so cold and wet."

In the middle of the night, a smudgy-looking kitten with its wet fur all standing up in spikes jumped on to Wanda's bed.

Wanda gently rubbed the kitten dry with a towel, rubbing away the rest of the dye.

"I don't really mind a ginger kitten," she said. "Maybe I can start a new fashion for witches."

NOSY GERALD GIRAFFE

Gerald was a very nosy giraffe. His long neck enabled him to bend his head to hear everything that was going on in the zoo.

Of course he couldn't help his long neck – and seeing what everyone was up to – but he *could* help being a terrible gossip.

Unfortunately, he just couldn't keep anything to himself. Nothing was ever a secret with Gerald around.

"I wish Gerald would hold his tongue," complained Percy the polar bear. "He'll make everyone unhappy the way he carries on."

Now, one day Gerald heard a commotion in the Parrot House. He wanted to find out what it was all about, and he had to stretch his long neck as far as it would go, and then tilt his head to the side to hear what was going on.

In fact, it wasn't very interesting after all: parrots are noisy birds at the best of times. Disappointed, Gerald pulled his neck back again but, to his horror, he found he had accidentally tied a knot in it!

Poor Gerald! He felt very, very uncomfortable, especially since the other animals all laughed at him. He looked so funny!

"It serves you right!" they said. "That will teach you to gossip so much!"

The zoo vet managed to untie Gerald's neck eventually, and it was soon perfectly all right again.

But Gerald had learned his lesson. He didn't stretch his neck out to hear private conversations any more. And if by chance he did happen to hear anything interesting, he certainly never gossiped about it.

PONY FOR SALE

Hazelnut had been Debbie's pony for five years, but now Debbie was too big to ride her.

"We have to find you a new home, Hazelnut," said Debbie sadly, giving Hazelnut a hug. "I need a pony I can ride and we can't afford to keep two."

After that, lots of strangers came to see Hazelnut, look at her teeth and her hooves, and run their hands down her back and legs. One little boy gave her sugar-lumps and whispered kindly in her ear. His mother helped him mount and he rode Hazelnut carefully round the field. Hazelnut liked him.

But the boy's mother shook her head.

"I'm afraid she's too expensive for us, Chris," she said.

Then another child came to look at Hazelnut. She didn't give her any sugar-lumps or try to ride her, but jumped up and down and cried, "Daddy! That's the pony for me. I want her."

"Are you sure, Annabel?" said the girl's father. "She's rather expensive."

Annabel stamped her foot.

"I *want* her! You said I could have any pony I liked! You *said*."

"Very well, sweetheart."

He wrote out a cheque and Hazelnut had a new home.

She had a splendid stable, plenty of feed and fresh water, and she should have been happy. But she wasn't.

Annabel, Hazelnut's new owner, was horribly spoilt. She treated Hazelnut very badly and was very unkind.

"You stupid pony!" she'd yell, if Hazelnut did something wrong.

One day, in a really bad fit of temper, Annabel started hitting poor Hazelnut with her riding crop. Annabel's mother came up and took the crop away.

"Hazelnut is going back," she told her furious daughter. "And you can't have another pony till you've learned to control your temper!"

And so Hazelnut found herself back in her old paddock once more.

Chris and his mother came back to see her.

"We want to be sure Hazelnut goes to a really good home this time," said Debbie's mother. "And that's more important than getting the price we wanted for her."

Before long, Chris was happily riding Hazelnut down the lane.

"You're my very first and best pony, Hazelnut," he said.

THE TALENT CONTEST

One day the animals in the jungle decided to hold a talent contest. Each animal had to say what it could do best, and the winner would be the animal judged most useful.

Monkey went first.

"I can swing from tree to tree," he said, "hang by my tail and throw a coconut a hundred metres."

"That sounds a bit dangerous," said Zebra. So it was decided that Monkey's skills weren't much use at all.

"I can squirt a jet of water two hundred metres," said Elephant, and demonstrated. Unfortunately he soaked everyone, so he was disqualified too.

"I can run like the wind," said Gazelle, but the judges decided that her talent wasn't much use to anyone but herself.

"I can sing beautifully," said Parrot. But no one else agreed with him.

Tiger was disqualified, too. His only talent seemed to be hunting the other animals.

Crocodile was next.

"I can pretend to be a log floating in the river," he said.

No one was sure that this was useful.

Suddenly there was a rumble of thunder and rain fell in torrents. All the animals ran for shelter, and soon the river washed away the wooden log bridge.

"What shall I do?" said Porcupine. "My children are trapped on the other side of the river. I can't get across."

"You can walk across on my back," said Crocodile.

"Can I come, too?" asked a little mouse.

Soon half a dozen small creatures had climbed on to Crocodile's back and they all safely crossed the river.

"Well, I think we've found the winner of the contest," said Elephant, and the others all agreed. Crocodile had certainly proved to be the most useful animal.

MAX THE CIRCUS LION

Max the circus lion looked very big and fierce, but he was really very gentle. His trainer, Jimmy Bravo, could even put his head safely inside Max's mouth.

To everyone in the circus, Max was just a big, soppy pussycat.

Some days, though, Max wished he could get out of his cage and be free, like a wild lion.

One day it happened. Jimmy didn't fasten Max's cage properly and the clever lion escaped. He hid under a caravan until he was sure no one would see him, then he bounded away into the nearby woods.

It smelled lovely and wild there. Max gave a happy rumble in his throat.

And somebody heard him.

Not far away a family was enjoying a picnic. As Mum poured tea out of the thermos flask, she lifted her head.

"Listen," she said. "I thought I heard something."

Little Susie got up and tiptoed over to the bushes. At the same time, Max poked his head through them. He could smell delicious sandwiches.

"Aargh! Help!" yelled Susie. "A lion!"

Max saw the lovely picnic spread out on the ground. He purred loudly and padded across the clearing to meet his new friends.

But of course the family thought Max was going to eat *them*. They ran off, crying, "Help! Police!"

Max helped himself to the food and then lay down in the sun for a nap. But he had barely closed his eyes when suddenly there were sirens, and people shouting, all round him.

"Don't get too near!" said a voice over a loudspeaker. "He's a wild and dangerous animal!"

Max got to his feet. All the strange noises were making him very anxious.

Then he heard a familiar voice.

"Put those guns away at once. He's my lion, and he's not at all dangerous."

And into the clearing strode Jimmy Bravo!

Max was very pleased to see him.

"Poor old Max," said Jimmy, rubbing his shaggy head. "You just wanted some freedom, didn't you? Well I've news for you. You and I are going to a safari park."

Now Max has his freedom and Jimmy Bravo still looks after him. Sometimes, to amuse the tourists in the park, Jimmy puts his head into Max's huge mouth – just to remind them both of the old days.

BURGLARS

The holiday cottage was in a peaceful spot, overlooking the sea. It was not the kind of place you'd expect to find burglars. That was what Tom thought, until he heard the noises in the night.

When he went to bed that evening, he fell asleep thinking of the rock pools he was going to explore next day.

What was that? Tom woke very suddenly with a thumping heart. Someone was making a noise outside the back door.

He was sure they were trying to break in. He crept out of bed and went to his parents' room.

"Mum! Dad! Wake up!" said Tom, shaking Dad's shoulder. "There are burglars!"

"What?" Dad sat up in bed and felt for the heavy rubber torch, which was usually kept in the car.

"Stay here, Tom," said his dad, and he went quietly downstairs.

"Be careful, Dave," said Mum, watching from the landing.

Tom went and peered out of his window, but it was very dark and he couldn't see very much: just something shadowy moving around.

Then Dad came upstairs again. He put his arms round Tom's shoulders.

"Look carefully, Tom, and keep still," he said. "You'll see your 'burglars' in a moment."

Just then the moon came out from behind a cloud – and Tom saw…

"Badgers! Wow!"

"They were raiding the dustbin," said Dad, laughing.

They all watched the badgers for a long time. Mum put out food for them after that and they came every night. But Dad tied down the dustbin lid. Those burglars could make a terrible mess otherwise!

TIMOTHY TORTOISE'S SPECIAL PATCH

Timothy Tortoise was very, very old. He'd lived in the same garden since before Harriet was born and he had his own favourite sunny patch behind the garden shed.

One warm and sunny spring day, Timothy woke up from his long winter's sleep and made his way contentedly to his special patch.

It wasn't there! Where the wild strawberries had once grown there was now a horrible stone patio with little plants growing between the cracks in the stones, but nothing Timothy liked to eat. He nibbled at one of the plants but it tasted horrible. The old shed had gone, too. There was a new, white building there instead, with glass walls.

Timothy went into his shell and sulked. Maybe when he looked out again, everything would be back exactly as it used to be.

When Harriet and Sam found him, not even a succulent lettuce leaf could tempt him out.

"I think he's sulking," said Sam. "It's because his special patch has gone."

Sam and Harriet ran to tell their parents.

"We'll just have to find him another patch," said Dad, putting on his gumboots.

They all went to the garden to search for a new patch for Timothy.

"How about my garden?" said Harriet.

The others laughed. Harriet's "garden" was famous. It was a wilderness of weeds and vegetables run to seed.

It was just the place for Timothy.

Harriet picked him up and put him gently down in the middle of it. She even brought out her doll's-house in place of the shed.

When Timothy finally came out of his shell, he was soon munching happily in his new home.

THE BIG OUTDOOR ADVENTURE

Percy and Polly were two mice who lived in an old attic. It was a wonderful place for mice, full of all kinds of junk, and it had a network of runs leading all over the house.

One day, when the two mice went to visit little Harry's room to look for biscuit crumbs, they discovered an enormous piece of cheese sitting on a block of wood by the skirting board.

"Oooh," cried Polly, drooling. But Percy caught hold of her tail.

"Don't go near it, Polly. It's a mouse-trap!" he said. "They know we are here. After the traps will come rat poison, and if we don't fall for that, then they'll get a cat."

Both mice felt very frightened, especially when people came into the attic next day and began to move the boxes.

"Ugh! Mice!" said the wife. "I'll put down some poison."

"Better to get a cat," said her husband.

The little mice trembled in their nest.

"What did I tell you?" said Percy. "It's just not safe here any more."

"Let's move," said Polly. "Cousin Matilda said there was plenty of room in the garden shed."

The very next night, Polly and Percy left their attic, scampered down the stairs, and squeezed under the back door, out into the garden.

It smelled very strange and exciting.

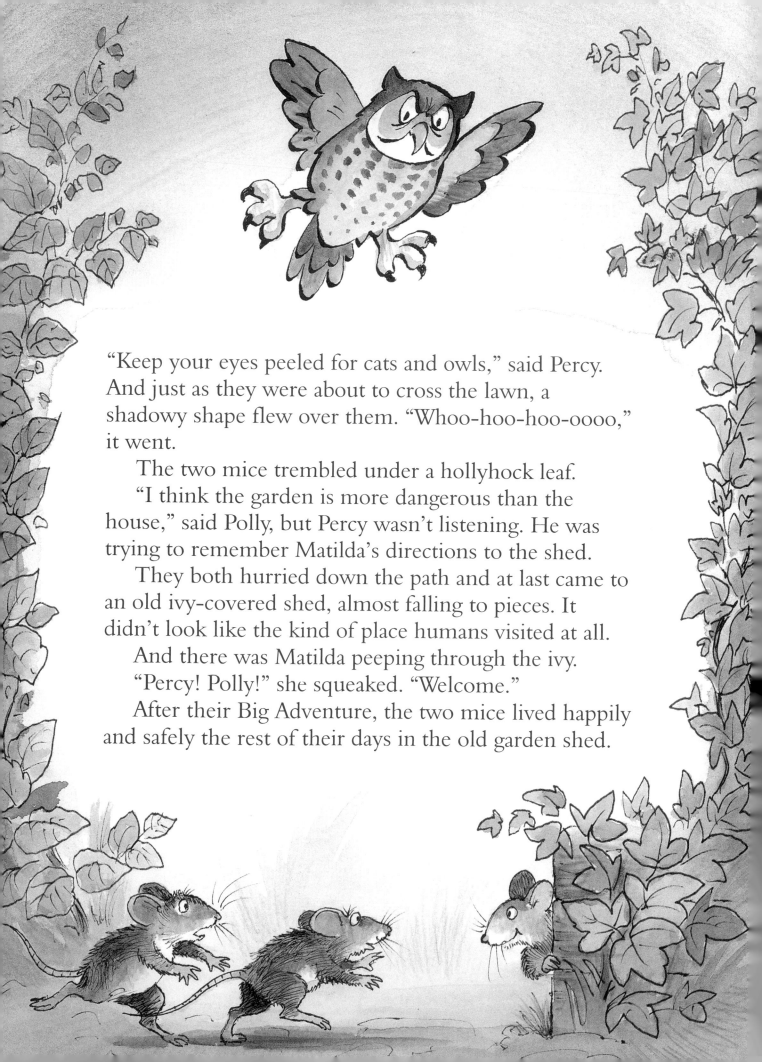

"Keep your eyes peeled for cats and owls," said Percy. And just as they were about to cross the lawn, a shadowy shape flew over them. "Whoo-hoo-hoo-oooo," it went.

The two mice trembled under a hollyhock leaf.

"I think the garden is more dangerous than the house," said Polly, but Percy wasn't listening. He was trying to remember Matilda's directions to the shed.

They both hurried down the path and at last came to an old ivy-covered shed, almost falling to pieces. It didn't look like the kind of place humans visited at all.

And there was Matilda peeping through the ivy.

"Percy! Polly!" she squeaked. "Welcome."

After their Big Adventure, the two mice lived happily and safely the rest of their days in the old garden shed.

CAT BURGLAR

Tufty Tabby Cat was a greedy thief. His family knew this, and were very careful about leaving food on the table, or on the kitchen counter. But not everyone in Chapel Street was aware of Tufty's bad habits.

Mrs Henshall at number 6 lost a roast chicken one day, which she had left near her kitchen window.

And Dan Davey's parcel of fish and chips disappeared from his shopping bag while he was unlocking the front door.

Tufty Tabby Cat was sneaky; no one ever caught him.

He was prowling around the block of flats one day when he suddenly smelled something delicious. He looked up and saw a plate of fresh liver on a windowsill three floors up.

Undismayed, Tufty looked around to see how he could climb up there.

There was a shed with a flat roof next to the block of flats. Tufty leaped on to the roof, and then across to the second-floor window ledge.

Now the window with the liver was immediately above him. There was a drainpipe one side, and Tufty clawed and scrambled his way up it, hauling himself up the brickwork with his claws.

He made it! Tufty reached the windowsill and snatched the liver right off the plate!

But then he had a problem. He found he couldn't climb down.

He could only jump across to the window ledge of the flat next door.

But there was another cat there: a fierce, black tomcat with spiky fur.

"Push off!" hissed the cat, arching his back.

Tufty dropped the liver in fright. It fell down on to the ground where a passing dog gobbled it up.

Poor Tufty couldn't escape!

In minutes he was shooed right down the stairs and into the street by the owner of the flat, who then threw a bucket of water after him. Soaked and with a nasty scratch on his nose and some fur missing here and there, Tufty limped home.

It was a long time before Tufty Tabby Cat was tempted to steal again.

PRISCILLA PIG

There was once a pig called Priscilla who thought she was the prettiest, most elegant and certainly the cleanest pig in the world. And she probably was, for she washed herself in the pond every day and polished her trotters till they shone.

Unfortunately for Priscilla, she had to share her sty with twelve other snorting, snuffling, grubby, vulgar pigs.

"I'm really far too fine to live with them," she said, wrinkling up her nose at her noisy companions who had their noses buried in the pig trough.

And she went to the pond for another dip.

One day the farmer came to the pigsty with a stranger. Priscilla had just had her wash and her pink body showed up beautifully against all the grime of the other pigs.

"That looks a fine pig," said the stranger, pointing at Priscilla. "I'll have that one."

When he had gone Priscilla was aglow with pride.

"He chose me," she boasted. "And do you know why?"

"Because you're the pinkest, most beautiful, cleanest and most elegant pig in the world," sang out the other pigs. Priscilla, of course, didn't realise they were all making fun of her.

"And the most stuck up," said a young piglet, but Priscilla pretended not to hear.

Then Sampson, the big boar, snorted at Priscilla. "You foolish pig!" he said. "You were picked out because you showed up the best. Do you know what happens to pigs that leave the sty?"

"I expect they go to a nice, new, clean home," said Priscilla, haughtily.

"Bacon. That's what," said Sampson. "You'll be turned into bacon!"

"Or sausages," said the piglet.

Priscilla trembled. She hadn't thought of that. She quickly jumped straight into a muddy puddle and rolled over and over until she looked exactly like the other pigs.

"Where's that pink pig?" asked the stranger when he returned. "Never mind – that one will do." And he picked up the cheeky young piglet.

As he turned away, Priscilla heard him say to the farmer, "We'll have to clean him up, though. Don't believe in putting dirty pigs into a brand-new, clean sty."

TOFI'S TRICK

Tofi was a very cheeky monkey who loved to play tricks on the other animals.

His favourite one was to drop over-ripe fruit on their heads from his tree. *Splat*! they would go and Tofi would fall about laughing.

Eli the elephant would squirt the naughty monkey with water, and Rambo the rhino would catch the squashy fruit on his horn.

But Samba the lion didn't find Tofi's tricks at all funny. It wasn't very dignified for the King of the Jungle to have rotten fruit flung at him.

"You just wait till I catch you!" he would roar at Tofi.

Tofi was far too nimble to be caught. He'd bound into the treetops, laughing his head off.

Except one day he was not so lucky.

He had dropped a squidgy mango on Samba's nose and was about to race away through the treetops to safety, when *crack*! – the branch he was on snapped and Tofi fell from the tree right on to Samba's back.

"Grrrrraahhh!" roared the angry lion, swishing his tail from side to side. "Now I'll get you!"

Tofi grabbed hold of Samba's fur and clung on tightly. After all, Samba couldn't eat him if he was on the lion's back.

However hard Samba shook himself, or ran through whippy bushes and galloped across the plain, Tofi managed to stay put and out of reach.

Eventually Samba stopped to drink at a water hole, and he crouched down to lap thirstily. So very gently and quietly Tofi jumped off the lion's back and sped away.

Samba gave a gigantic roar, but he didn't bother to run after the little monkey. He had given Tofi a Big Fright, and he knew that the cheeky little animal wouldn't be trying his tricks again – at least not on Samba!

"GARTH WILL GET YOU"

Garth was a huge gorilla who lived in a zoo. Because he looked so ferocious, especially when he beat his chest and roared, he was the most popular animal with the visitors. Even the children loved it when he lumbered up to the bars of his cage and glared at them.

He reminded them of their favourite scary horror film.

Parents would threaten, "Garth will get you!" when their children misbehaved.

Now one day, a naughty little boy found out how to undo Garth's cage door, and left it open. Garth lumbered out and began to explore the zoo.

"Garth the gorilla is coming!" shrieked the children, running in all directions.

"Help! Help!" yelled their parents. They gathered up the children, ran into the parrot house and slammed the door.

Garth sat down and looked around. Where was everyone? Where were all his friends?

Only one little girl remained. Daisy used to visit Garth every weekend. She didn't shiver with fright like the other children.

She would look into Garth's eyes and see that they were rather sad and very wise.

Now Daisy went up to Garth and put her arms round his big hairy neck.

"Ooh!" cried the people in the parrot house.

Garth gave Daisy a very gentle hug.

78

"He's crushing that little girl!" they shrieked.

"Don't be silly," said Daisy. "Can't you see that he's a gentle gorilla?"

Gradually, the visitors came out of their hiding places. When the keepers came to take Garth back to his cage, they found children and grown-ups crowding round Garth, stroking his back and rubbing his head.

Garth was very, very happy. After all, friends aren't really friends at all if they are scared of you!

TOWN SHEEP

Letty Lamb was born in a big city, in a town farm.

When she was a tiny lamb, she was a favourite with the schoolchildren who visited the farm. But once she had grown up, they lost interest in her.

They'd race past her to visit the ducklings or the donkeys.

Letty became very lonely.

She remembered the day when the children fed her from a bottle and cuddled her. But no one wanted to cuddle a full-grown, scruffy-looking sheep.

"What shall we do about you, eh, Letty?" said the manager of the farm one day. "We've got two new lambs coming tomorrow, and there's no room for all of you."

Letty knew the farm wouldn't want to keep an old sheep if it had two new lambs to attract the crowds.

She was very worried. What would happen to her now?

The manager saw her sad and worried expression.

"Tell you what, Letty, I've got a splendid idea. I'll just phone a friend…"

The very next day a small pick-up truck drew up at the farm and Letty was put into it.

"Now what?" she wondered.

After a very long journey, the pick-up truck stopped and the ramp was lowered.

"Come on, Letty," said the driver.

Letty smelled good, fresh air and appetising grass. It was very different from the city. She had arrived at a farm in the country.

You can imagine how different her life became. She could roam freely over a grassy hillside, finding the tastiest shoots to eat, and soon made friends with the other sheep, even if they did think it funny that Letty had never seen a green hill before.

Every spring, Letty's thick woolly coat was shorn and spun into wool to make beautiful clothes for people.

Sometimes other sheep would arrive from town farms, just like Letty, and she always tried to help them feel welcome. And though she missed all the children, Letty knew that here, deep in the country, was her real home.

LOTTIE LOST

"Mum! Mum! we can't find Lottie," cried Emma, bursting into the kitchen.

Mum banged Lottie's food bowl with a spoon. The little cat always came when she heard that, but this time she did not appear.

They searched everywhere. Mum and Emma listened at garages and sheds, in case Lottie had been shut inside, while Dad and Andrew went round the streets calling her. They put up notices all round the neighbourhood.

But no one had seen a black and white cat with a smudgy nose.

Andrew and Emma couldn't sleep, wondering what had happened to her.

By the end of the week, they didn't think they would ever see Lottie again.

Then they heard a strange story. Their neighbour, Mrs obinson, had been burgled on the day that Lottie disappeared. By a lucky chance, the police had found the thief sprawled at the roadside by his van, surrounded by broken, stolen video equipment.

"Fell over a bloomin' cat that sprang out of the van," he told them.

Emma wondered if the cat could have been Lottie. The van had been found fifty miles away, so if it *had* been Lottie, she must be now well and truly lost.

Three weeks later as it was getting dark and Mum was drawing the curtains, she suddenly cried out:

"Gracious! Look who's on our windowsill!"

It was Lottie. Thin and dirty but very much alive!

With a cry Andrew ran out of the door and gathered her in his arms.

"Could she really have walked that far?" said Emma. She looked at Lottie's little feet. They were very sore.

"I reckon you did," she said. "And you caught a burglar."

MRS CRABTREE'S COAT

Mrs Crabtree had a leopard-skin coat and matching hat. Nowadays, hardly anyone wears real fur because they don't like to think of animals being killed for the sake of fashion.

But it didn't worry Mrs Crabtree.

"I'd rather have a dead leopard on my back," she said, "than a live one. Ha ha."

And despite what people thought, Mrs Crabtree wore her fur coat and hat every time she went out.

"If people like you stopped buying real fur, no one would trap the poor animals any more," said her next-door neighbour.

"Mind your own business!" snapped Mrs Crabtree.

That afternoon Mrs Crabtree visited the zoo. As well as her fur coat and hat, she wore a pair of leopard-skin gloves and carried an expensive crocodile-skin handbag.

She paraded grandly among the visitors, pretending to admire the animals.

Then she came to the leopards' enclosure.

"Where are the leopards today?" she demanded rudely. "I can't see any."

"They're probably hiding," said the keeper, looking with distaste at Mrs Crabtree's outfit.

Then Mrs Crabtree noticed a leopard staring fiercely at her from behind a tree. She shivered.

Suddenly, she felt something uncomfortable happening to her coat. It was wriggling on her back! And her hat began clawing at her hair, swishing its tail round her face.

"Tail? My hat didn't have a tail," she thought in panic.

Now the fur coat was fighting to get away from her. Mrs Crabtree shook herself free, shutting her eyes in horror. When she opened them again, a real live leopard was standing beside her, licking its lips hungrily.

"Aaagh!" shrieked Mrs Crabtree, and she ran off down the path, coatless, hatless and gloveless. She just remembered to throw her crocodile handbag into the crocodile pool as she raced by. Otherwise, goodness knows what would have happened.

UNWISE OWL

When Mrs Owl read Sam's school report, she gasped.

"Bottom of the class!" she exclaimed. "Can't add up," she read. "Can't remember the date of the Great Owl War," and so on.

Mr Owl was even more upset. "After generations of wise old owls, we have you – an unwise owl."

The truth was that Sam found school lessons very boring. What was the point of learning dates, or counting to ten, when an owl was supposed to catch mice? Sam was very good at that.

His father never caught his own mice: he spent his time giving advice to other animals and in return they provided food for the Owl family.

That was until Mr Owl lost his voice. He couldn't even say "*Whoo*?" And he certainly couldn't give any advice to anyone.

Mrs Owl didn't know what to do: since marrying Mr Owl, she'd never had to hunt for food, but she was very good at preparing what the other animals brought her.

A whole queue of animals had to be turned away because Mr Owl couldn't speak to them.

This meant that the larder was becoming very bare.

"I can help!" said Sam.

"You can't even spell 'harvest mouse'," said Mrs Owl, feeling hungry and irritable. "How can you possibly help?"

"This is my chance," thought Sam as he spread his wings and flew silently over the wood. Just as silently he swooped down and caught a mouse.

When he returned at suppertime, Sam laid a dozen mice proudly in front of his parents.

"Clever Sam," said his mother.

Mr Owl clicked his beak. "Can you tell me how many mice you have caught, Sam?" he just managed to croak.

"Eight?" guessed Sam. "Fifteen?"

"He's not clever," wheezed Mr Owl. "He's a dimwit. A wise owl knows how to count."

But Sam, happily eating his supper, knew he was wiser and cleverer than either of them.

HOPPITY HARRIET

It seemed to Harriet, the kangaroo, that she was the only animal in their small zoo that didn't do anything interesting.

Oliver Elephant gave the children rides.

Clarissa Chimp held funny tea parties.

And Solomon Seal did the most amazing tricks.

But poor Harriet did nothing but hoppity-hop around her enclosure.

One day Mr Jolly – who owned the zoo – came to Harriet, looking very worried.

"Oliver is not feeling well enough to give rides," he said. "And unless I can offer the children something interesting, they won't want to come. These days they want theme parks and roller-coasters." Then suddenly Mr Jolly had a brilliant idea.

"How would you like to give the children rides?" he asked Harriet.

"How?" said Harriet, astonished. "They'd all slide off my back!"

"Not on your back, silly!" said Mr Jolly. He explained what he meant. Harriet thought it was a lovely idea.

Very soon a queue of very small children was lined up waiting for a ride… in Harriet's pouch!

Hoppity-hop went Harriet, all round the zoo, and the little children she carried shrieked with excitement. Sometimes she jumped so high that they thought they were flying. It was better than a roller-coaster!

And when Oliver was well again, he carried on giving rides to the bigger children and their parents, but Harriet hopped with the tiny tots.

It was the only zoo in the country that gave kangaroo rides! Harriet was happy at last.

MAD MARCH HARE DAY

One bright spring morning, Mrs Squirrel looked out of her bedroom window.

"Oh, no!" she groaned.

Running wildly round the lawn, kicking up lumps of turf, was Harry Hare.

Before Mrs Squirrel could call out, Harry leaped over the gate. There was a clatter and a crash and the sound of broken glass as Harry crashed into the milk float.

Mr Badger the milkman shook his fist at the long-legged figure disappearing round the bend like lightning.

"No milk today," said Mr Badger, sweeping up the mess of broken bottles and milk.

"No lessons today," said Miss Goat the teacher, when she saw the havoc Harry had caused at Pepperpot School. Desks were overturned and all the exercise books were covered in powder paint.

"No school!" cried all the animal children, delighted. They ran off to fly their kites.

But Harry hadn't finished. He ran through Mrs Fox's garden, breaking her washing-line and tossing clean clothes everywhere.

He ran right in front of the Reverend Tabbycat's bicycle, making the vicar swerve into a ditch.

He splashed into the village pond, scattering ducks and frogs in all directions.

P.C. Doberman caught up with Harry just as the sun was setting. He marched him off and shut him in a cell at the police station.

"You can come out now, Harry," he said next morning.

A very confused Harry crept out of the police cell.

"What am I doing here?" he asked.

Can you believe it? Harry couldn't remember a single thing about the chaos he caused the day before.

"Something must have come over me," he said faintly, when P.C. Doberman told him what he'd done.

"Yes," said the policeman. "Yesterday was the First of March. Mad March Hare Day!"

THE SCHOOL PET

"Mum, can we look after the school pet during the holidays?" asked Scott when he came home from school.

"I should think so," said his mother, thinking that a little hamster or rabbit would be rather fun.

"Great!" said Scott, and the next morning he gave his teacher the good news.

"Well," said his teacher. "Lucy is taking the gerbils. And James is having the rabbit. And Kylie wants to look after the guinea pigs."

"*Oh*," said Scott.

"Which leaves Humphrey."

"*Oh*," said Scott again. Humphrey was the school goat. "I expect Mum won't mind."

But when Scott's mother saw Scott leading Humphrey through the gate she nearly had a fit. Especially as Humphrey was helping himself to the roses.

"Scott!" she gasped. "What on earth is *that*!"

"It's Humphrey," said Scott cheerfully. "He's the school pet we're looking after."

Humphrey munched on a tub of petunias.

Scott's mother groaned. Why hadn't she asked what the pet would be?

"Tie him to the apple tree for now," she said. "I'll have to think what to do with him."

Scott was sent out into the garden to make sure that Humphrey didn't eat the washing, while his mother went out to do her shopping at the supermarket.

"What do goats eat?" she wondered. "Apart from roses and petunias."

She was gone for some time. When she finally drove her car up the drive, Humphrey had managed to eat half a row of onions as well, before Scott could stop him.

A small van pulled up behind Scott's mother and the Vicar's wife got out.

"I met the Vicar's wife in the supermarket, Scott," his mum said cheerfully. "Humphrey's going to stay in the Vicarage orchard. He can keep the grass down for them and eat all the windfall apples. She's going to take him back there now."

"Who's a lucky goat, then?" said Scott.

Humphrey just burped.